The BINS of COTTERIDGE DOWN

Peta Lemon   Maria Dasic Todoric

This book is dedicated to life's unsung heroes, the common street bins. Keep up the good work!

Quirky
Picture
Press

In a corner of England lies an old town.
A curious place.
It's called Cotteridge Down.

The streets are so clean that they sparkle and shine.
The children all walk in a sensible line.

The most helpful people you'll ever meet
Make sure that there's never dirt on the street.

But Cotteridge Down wasn't always this way.
It's all because of what happened one day......

When Cotteridge Down was not at all clean.
But the smelliest, dirtiest place ever seen.

Festering rubbish was left on the ground.
Filthy old carpets and boots lay around.

Things flung out the window.

Pinged out the door.

Nobody used the bins anymore.

The smell was revolting! Too much to bear.
Even the rats packed and left in despair.

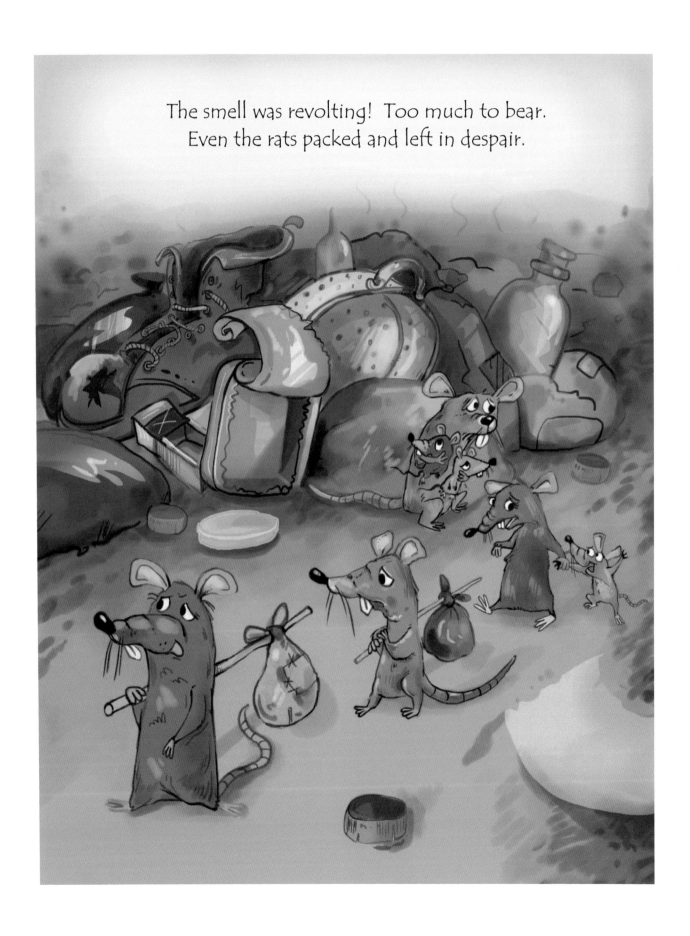

Fed up and cross with the state of the place,
an empty street bin said,

It called a midnight meeting
with the bins under the bridge.
To make a plan to put things right,
by an upturned fridge.

How dare they ruin Cotteridge Down?
The bins were all irate.
An uprising was needed
before it was too late!

The bins all hatched a plan
then headed home to bed.

No longer would they stand and watch
but do something instead.

Morning came. The plan began.
These bins were on a mission.
To carry out the greatest cleaning expedition!

3 …. 2 … 1 …. Go! The bins set off.
It was time to put things right.
Swerving corners as they raced at the speed of light.

They went for those who'd made the mess,
who'd started now to run.
But they were picked up in a flash
and plonked in one by one.

Filthy Phil and Fred were caught as they tried to hide.

They had spent the last week spitting milkshake on the slide.

And Johnny Gruffs, the builder,
who'd made the grave mistake.

Of fly-tipping his rubbish
every day into the lake.

Grumpy Mrs. Grobble
was picked up by her dress.

She had never bothered
to pick up her dogs' mess.

And finally, a bin spun round
and scooped up naughty Claire.

For sticking her blue bubble gum
on that lady's chair.

In half an hour the job was done. The bins had caught the lot.
Everyone who'd made such mess,
up to their necks in grot.

The bins paraded what they'd caught
in the longest line you've seen.
Then headed off to London
so they could show the Queen.

The news crews came out in their droves.
This story must be told!

And people all around the
world watched this
all unfold.

As they passed through crowds
they were greeted with a cheer.
And when the bins saw their support
they shed a little tear.

The Queen was most impressed!
And gave the Royal wave.
Her guardsmen gave them a salute.
Because they'd been so brave.

"Thanks for stopping by.
I hope you all can see.
That now you have to put things right,"
the Queen said cheerily.

Those in bins agreed.
They'd caused a dreadful mess.
So hurried home to clean it up.
Expedition a success!

From then on
Cotteridge Down turned round
to how it is today.

Memories of those in bins
have never gone away.

So if you ever think
you might drop a thing or two...

Can you be quite sure
that a bin's not watching you?

Printed in Great
Britain
by Amazon